W9-BMI-969 11/2011

ANIMAL ANTICS A TO Z.

Xavier Ox's Xylophone Experiment

by Barbara deRubertis • illustrated by R.W. Alley

THE KANE PRESS / NEW YORK

Alpha Betty's Class

Alexander Anteater

Bobby Baboon

Corky Cub

Dilly Dog

Eddie Elephant

Frances Frog

Gertie Gorilla

Hanna Hippo

Izzy Impala

Jeremy Jackrabbit

Kylie Kangaroo

Lana Llama

Maxwell Moose

Nina Nandu

Oliver Otter

Polly Porcupine

Quentin Quokka

Rosie Raccoon

Sammy Skunk

Tessa Tiger

Umma Ungka

Victor Vicuna

Walter Warthog

STAR
of the
BOOK

Xavier Ox

Yoko Yak

Zachary Zebra

Alpha Betty

Library of Congress Cataloging-in-Publication Data

deRubertis, Barbara.
Xavier Ox's xylophone experiment / by Barbara deRubertis ; illustrated by R.W. Alley.
p. cm. — (Animal antics A to Z)
Summary: Xavier Ox is a wonderful musician when he arrives at Alpha Betty's school,
so when his home-made drum set falls apart Alpha Betty and his classmates experiment
with building him an extra-strong xylophone.
ISBN 978-1-57565-357-0 (library binding : alk. paper) — ISBN 978-1-57565-349-5 (pbk. : alk. paper) —
ISBN 978-1-57565-388-4 (e-book)
[1. Musicians—Fiction. 2. Schools—Fiction. 3. Oxen—Fiction. 4. Animals—Fiction. 5. Alphabet.]
I. Alley, R. W. (Robert W.), ill. II. Title.
PZ7.D4475Xav 2011
[E]—dc22   2010051472

1 3 5 7 9 10 8 6 4 2

First published in the United States of America in 2011 by Kane Press, Inc.
Printed in the United States of America
WOZ0711

Series Editor: Juliana Hanford
Book Design: Edward Miller

Animal Antics A to Z is a registered trademark of Kane Press, Inc.

www.kanepress.com

Xavier Ox LOVED music.

As soon as he could talk, he started to sing.
As soon as he could walk, he started to dance.

To make the music extra exciting, he would
bang on pots and pans!

So Xavier's parents tied six boxes
together to make him a drum set.

And Xavier made shakers by filling
two little boxes with beans.

Now Xavier could play the drums while he sang.
And he could shake the shakers while he danced.

By the time Xavier came to Alpha Betty's school,
he was an excellent musician!

One day at school, Alpha Betty taught
her class the alphabet song.

Xavier sang along. He also snapped his
fingers and tapped his toes.
"Go, Xavier!" exclaimed Alpha Betty.

The next day, Xavier brought his drum set to school.

"May I play during the alphabet song?" he asked.

"Please do!" said Alpha Betty.

Xavier's sticks went clickity-clack-clack and
bippity-bop-bop on the boxes.

It was so exciting, the class stopped singing.
They watched Xavier's drumming explosion!

Xavier became more and more excited.
His sticks pounded. The boxes bounced.
And bits of the boxes flew everywhere!

When Xavier finished, he was exhausted!

"Oh, my!" said Alpha Betty. "You get lots of
EXERCISE when you play the alphabet song!"

She examined the broken boxes. "These can't
be fixed, Xavier. You are a very strong little ox.
So you need a stronger musical instrument!
Let's think about it. Then we can experiment."

After recess, Alpha Betty showed Xavier
a picture. "Look at this xylophone!" she said.

"Wow!" said Xavier. "How much does it cost?"

"Six hundred dollars," said Alpha Betty.

"That's too expensive!" Xavier whispered.

Alpha Betty smiled. "Exactly. But we could experiment with *making* a xylophone!"

"That would be GREAT!" Xavier exclaimed.

Alpha Betty explained the experiment to the class.
She read a list of supplies they would need:

"Boards to make the box,

extra-strong wood for the bars,

pegs, felt, sandpaper, glue . . . and tools."

"We need a LOT of stuff," Xavier said nervously.

Alexander Anteater raised his hand first.
"I can bring boards to make a box!"

Maxwell Moose quickly added, "I'll explore
in the woods with my mom. We can find
extra-strong wood for the bars there!"

Rosie Raccoon jumped up. "You'll need two mallets, Xavier. I'll make them tonight!"

"And I'll bring my toolbox," said Alpha Betty.

Xavier grinned. "I can take care of all the extras."

Then he shouted, "Thank you, everyone!"

The class arrived at school early the next day.
They were excited about the xylophone
experiment!

First, Alpha Betty sawed the wood into
bars of different lengths.

Next, she helped Xavier make a box.
He carefully laid the bars across it.

"Now our music expert needs to test the
tones," said Alpha Betty.

Xavier flexed his arms.
Then he pounded away with the two mallets.

The xylophone seemed to explode!
Bars bounced off the box and flew into the air!
The class ran for cover!

Alpha Betty shook her head and smiled.
"Test the tones *softly*, Xavier," she said.
"We'll fix the bars in place later."

So Xavier *gently* tapped each bar.
"The tones are exactly right!" he exclaimed.

Now the whole class pitched in to help Xavier.
They finished sanding the wood bars.
They glued pegs and felt to the box.

Alpha Betty said the glue would be dry
by morning. The xylophone was
almost complete!

In bed that night, Xavier closed his eyes.
He hummed. He wiggled his toes to the beat.
And he practiced playing the alphabet song
on an imaginary xylophone.

The next day, the xylophone was ready.

All the students gathered around Xavier.
First he softly, slowly tapped out the tune to
the alphabet song.

Then he played it in a louder, bouncier way!
The class happily began to sing along.

Suddenly they heard an unexpected sound. . . .

Someone was playing along on a saxophone!

It was Alpha Betty!

The class exploded with excitement!

Alexander Anteater stood on his hands.
Bobby Baboon be-bopped. Dilly Dog danced.
And Xavier Ox played his xylophone like an expert!

It was the most EXCITING performance of the
alphabet song . . . EVER!

When they finished, they fell to the floor.
They were all exhausted . . . all except
Xavier Ox.

"Thank you, everyone!" Xavier exclaimed.
"Our experiment worked!
The xylophone is EXCELLENT!
The saxophone player is EXCEPTIONAL!"

"And . . . ," Xavier Ox grinned,
"we'll all get LOTS of extra exercise
whenever we sing the alphabet song!"

FUN FACTS

- **Home:** Musk oxen are native to the Arctic areas of North America. They lived at the same time as the woolly mammoth! But unlike the mammoths, musk oxen were able to survive the last ice age.
- **Size:** An adult musk ox is usually about 4 feet high at the shoulder. It weighs about 600 pounds, on average.
- **Appearance:** All musk oxen have large heads, humped shoulders, and shaggy coats. Their long, heavy, downward-curving horns also form a protective helmet on top of their heads!
- **Did You Know?** When a herd of musk oxen is threatened, the bulls and cows form a circle or semicircle around the calves and face outward!

LOOK BACK

Learning to identify letter sounds (phonemes) at the beginning, middle, and end of words is called "phonemic awareness."

- *X* can make two different sounds. When a word <u>begins</u> with the letter *x*, it makes the *z* sound—like **xylophone**.
- When *x* is found in the <u>middle</u> or at the <u>end</u> of a word, it makes the usual *x* sound (*ks*)—like **ox**.
- Listen to the words on page 15 being read again. If you hear *x* making the *z* sound at the <u>beginning</u> of a word, repeat the word and extend the *z* sound when you repeat it! (For example, "ZZZ-avier!")
- Listen to the words on page 13 being read again. When you hear a word that contains the *x* sound (*ks*), cross your arms into an "X" in front of you and repeat the *x* sound three times: "*x-x-x*" ("*ks-ks-ks*").

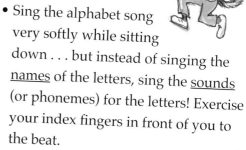

TRY THIS!

Exercise While Singing the Alphabet Song!

- Sing the alphabet song very softly while sitting down . . . but instead of singing the <u>names</u> of the letters, sing the <u>sounds</u> (or phonemes) for the letters! Exercise your index fingers in front of you to the beat.
- Now sing LOUDLY! Put your hands on your hips and march around the room in a circle while you sing the letter sounds.

WHEW! Now you've had some extra exercise—just like Xavier Ox!

FOR MORE ACTIVITIES, go to Xavier Ox's website: www.kanepress.com/AnimalAntics/XavierOx.html
You'll also find a recipe for Xavier Ox's Extra-Special Pancakes!